B55 082 152 2

KU-681-668

This **Walker** book
belongs to:

Rotherham Libraries

B55 082 152 2

PETERS	12-Jul-2022
	7.99
CHILD	RTMAL

A Note to Grown-ups

One day, I watched my youngest child getting angry – and I decided to write
a poem about it, which has now been turned into this picture book.
I wanted to explore the idea that anger takes over the whole world, because,
when you're very little, being angry is in part about wishing you were bigger.

By gently laughing at one of these big rages, I hope a child will see their
tantrum alongside that of the character in this book – and understand that,
even if anger can feel terrifyingly BIG, it doesn't usually last long!

For Emma, Elsie, Emile and Joni. M.R.

For Elsie. R.S.

First published 2021 by Walker Books Ltd, 87 Vauxhall Walk, London SE11 5HJ

This edition published 2022

2 4 6 8 10 9 7 5 3 1

Text © 2021 Michael Rosen • Illustrations © 2021 Robert Starling

The right of Michael Rosen and Robert Starling to be identified as author and illustrator respectively of this work has
been asserted by them in accordance with the Copyright, Designs and Patents Act 1988

This work has been typeset in Futura T

Printed in China

All rights reserved.
No part of this book may be reproduced, transmitted or stored in an information
retrieval system in any form or by any means, graphic, electronic or
mechanical, including photocopying, taping and recording,
without prior written permission from the publisher

British Library Cataloguing in Publication Data:
a catalogue record for this book is available from the British Library

ISBN 978-1-5295-0414-9

www.walker.co.uk

I AM ANGRY

Michael Rosen

ILLUSTRATED BY
Robert Starling

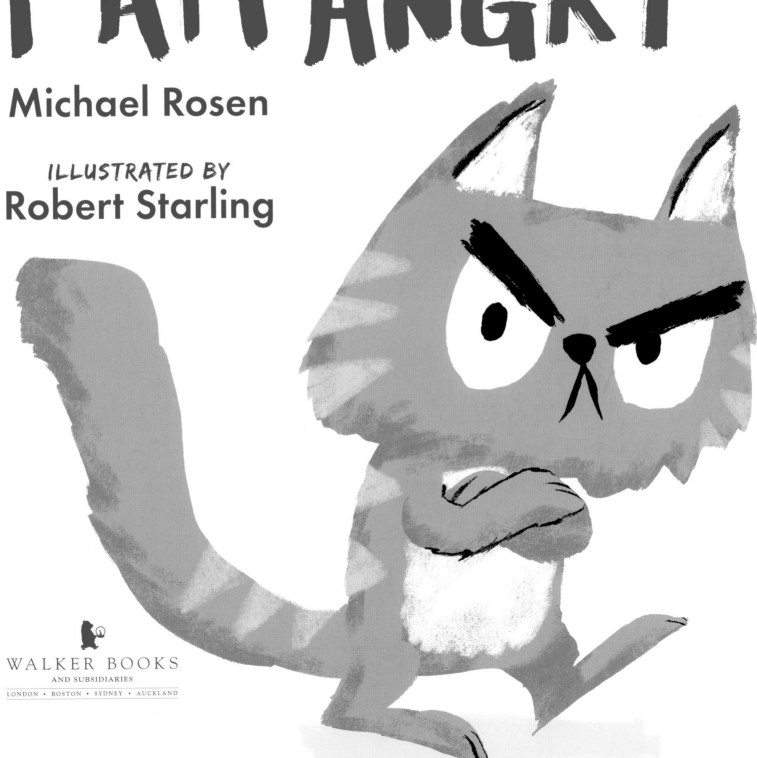

WALKER BOOKS
AND SUBSIDIARIES
LONDON • BOSTON • SYDNEY • AUCKLAND

I'm so angry, I'll ...

up

jump   and

down,

roll on the ground,

make a **din,**

make you spin,

throw you in the bin!

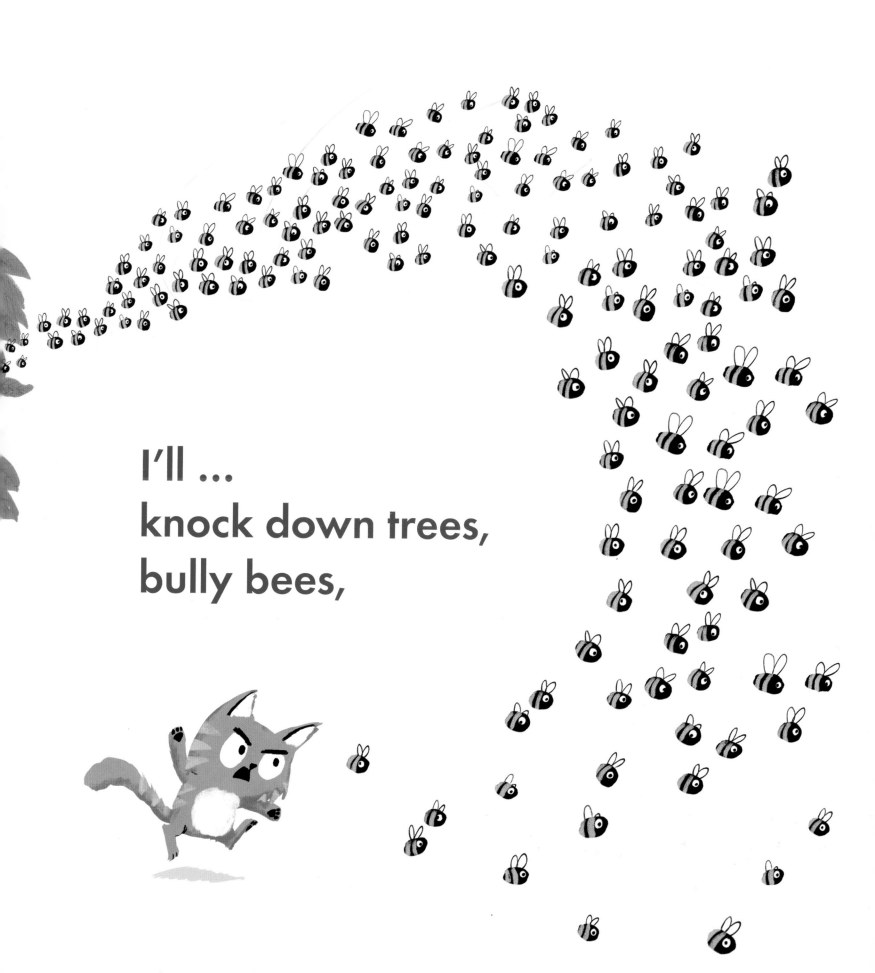

I'll ...
knock down trees,
bully bees,

scare spiders,

scare tigers,

ROAR!

(MIAOW)

catch cockatoos,

confuse
kangaroos!

I'll ... **bang** all the bones, **smash** up stones,

silence birds ...

mash up names,

grind up games,

burst a balloon,

squash the moon,

make
giants
run,

terrify the **sun,**

turn the sky red ...

and go to bed.